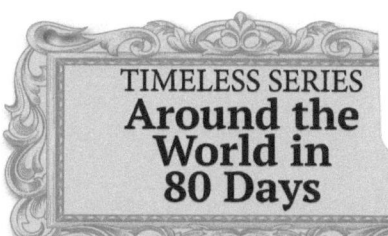

TIMELESS SERIES
Around the World in 80 Days

MAPLE KIDS

TIMELESS SERIES AROUND THE WORLD IN 80 DAYS

Published by

MAPLE PRESS PRIVATE LIMITED
office: A-63, Sector 58, Noida 201301, U.P., India
phone: +91 120 455 3581, 455 3583
email: info@maplepress.co.in
website: www.maplepress.co.in

Reprinted in 2019

ISBN: 978-93-50337-23-3

Contents

New Servant of Mr. Fogg

It was in the year 1872. Phileas Fogg lived at No.7, Saville Row, Burlington Garden in London. A member of the Reform Club, he was never seen at the Bank nor at the Exchange. He was neither a public employee nor a merchant or a manufacturer. In fact, little was known of his past and the source of his wealth. However, Mr. Fogg's cheques were always paid on time. It was likely that he had travelled a great deal but those who knew him closely, said that for the past many years Mr. Fogg had remained in London.

Mr. Fogg was not known to have a wife or any children. Nor was he known to have any relatives or close friends. Many people found that strange about him. He lived in his lavish home in Saville Row all by himself and was attended to by a single butler.

Though life at Saville Row was quite comfortable, Mr. Fogg expected his butler to be superhumanly active and exact. On 2nd October, he had dismissed James Foster, for the poor lad had brought him his shaving-water two degrees below the required temperature. Mr. Fogg was now expecting to hire

someone new and this person was expected to arrive between eleven and half past today.

Exactly at half past eleven every day, Mr. Fogg would leave his place and visit the Reform Club. As he was waiting in his parlour someone knocked at his door, and James announced the arrival of the new butler.

A thirty-year-old man advanced and bowed. "You are a Frenchman, I believe," asked Phileas Fogg, "and your name is John?"

"Jean, if monsieur pleases," he replied. His name was Jean Passepartout and he indeed was a Frenchman.

Jean Passepartout's unusual surname was due to the reason that he had often changed his job. He had been a singer, a circus-rider, a professor of gymnastics and a Sergeant-Fireman. He had left Paris some five years ago and had been a valet in England since then. He had heard that Mr. Fogg was the most exact and settled gentleman in the United Kingdom. Thus, in the hope of finally living in peace, he had come to Saville Row to attend to Mr. Fogg as his butler.

Mr. Fogg was impressed but he was apprehensive about whether Passepartout was aware of the conditions that the position held.

"What time is it?" asked Fogg. Passepartout pulled out a silver watch from his pocket and said that it was twenty-two minutes past eleven.

"You are too slow," said Fogg. Passepartout was puzzled.

"You are four minutes too slow. However, from this moment that is twenty-six minutes after eleven a.m., this Wednesday 2nd October, you are under my service." Fogg got up, took his hat and gently shut the front door behind him.

Passepartout noticed that his master was forty years of age, tall, well-built and had fine features. He seemed to be a very polished gentleman. Mr. Fogg was so exact that he was never in a hurry and was always ready. He never reached his destination before time nor was he ever late. And he was equally precise in his emotions. He never seemed to be moved or agitated.

As for Passepartout, he was an honest and pleasant fellow. He was strong, well-built and lively. Now alone in the house he began to thoroughly examine the mansion. The mansion was clean and well-arranged. This impressed him. His own living quarters were on the second storey. On the mantel in his room stood an electric clock, similar to the one in Mr. Fogg's bedchamber, both beating the same second at the same instant. Over the clock hung a card, which carried a time-table of Mr. Fogg's daily activities and instructions for the servant accordingly.

Mr. Fogg's World Trip

Everyday, Mr. Fogg visited the posh Reform Club in Pall Mall. After breakfast, at thirteen minutes to one he would rise and enter a large reading room. He would occupy himself with *The Times* and then *The Standard* until it was time for dinner. After dinner, he would return and sit down to the Pall Mall.

At around seven Fogg was joined by his usual partners at whist - Andrew Stuart, an engineer; John Sullivan and Sammuel Fallentin, bankers; Thomas Flanagan, a brewer and Gauthier Ralph, director of the Bank of England - in the reading room. They were all rich and respected men of London.

Today they discussed about a recent case of robbery. Flanagan began, "So Ralph, what about the robbery?" To this Stuart said, "The bank is going to lose the money." But Ralph was optimistic.

"Detectives have been sent to the major ports of America and Europe and it would be difficult for the robbers to get through them," he said; "*The Daily Telegraph* seemed to have the description of the robber as one pertaining to a gentleman.

The newspaper said that he was polished and seemed pretty well-to-do."

The robbery had occurred three days ago at the Bank of England. A sum of 55,000 pounds had been stolen from the main cashier's table. It was understood that the thief was perhaps not a professional since he had appeared like a gentleman. Stuart quite firmly believed that the thief might escape.

"The world is big enough," said Stuart. "It was once," retorted Phileas Fogg. Ralph agreed, "Certainly. The world has grown smaller, since a man can now go round it ten times more quickly than a hundred years ago. And that is why the search for this thief will be more likely to succeed."

However, Stuart was not convinced. "You have a strange way of proving that the world is now a smaller place than it used to be. Just because a man can travel around it in three months doesn't make it so."

"In eighty days, to be precise," said Mr. Fogg to everyone's astonishment.

As the rest of them wondered, Sullivan produced an estimate published in *The Daily Telegraph*, which conclusively said that the world could be travelled in 80 days.

Sullivan loudly read out the tabulation:
"London to Suez
(rail and steam boats) 7 days
Suez to Bombay (Steamer) 13 days

Bombay to Calcutta (rail)	3	days
Calcutta to Hong Kong (Steamer)	13	days
Hong Kong to Yokohama (Steamer)	6	days
Yokohama to San Francisco (Steamer)	22	days
San Francisco to New York (rail)	7	days
New York to London (Steamer and rail)	9	days
Total	80	days

"Does it include accidents and bad weather?" Stuart asked and Fogg assured him that it did.

"I'd like to see you do it. I'd bet four thousand pounds that such a journey is impossible," said Stuart.

"I'd bet my deposit of twenty thousand pounds at Barrings that it isn't," said Fogg coolly.

"It's absurd!" cried Stuart, but Fogg was quite firm about it. Thus, Stuart, Fallentin, Sullivan, Flanagan and Ralph after consulting amongst themselves, accepted the bet.

"Good," said Fogg. "The train leaves for Dover at a quarter before nine. I will take it. I shall be back in this very room on Saturday, the twenty-first day of December at a quarter before nine or else you may have the money. Here is a cheque of the amount." And he left the Reform Club to get ready and set off.

Much to Passepartout's surprise, Phileas Fogg returned home early that day. Mr. Fogg told his servant to get ready as they were to leave for a trip.

"We shall carry nothing more than just two carpet bags and shall buy our clothes on the way," said Fogg. Passepartout was shocked out of his wits. Was his master a fool? Travel around the world in eighty days? Was it even possible? But he obeyed his master as was his duty.

Fogg consulted the 'Bracshaw's continental Railway steam Transit and General Guide', and slipped into a bag, a fat roll of notes from the Bank of England.

They locked the house and took a cab to Charing Cross. On the way much to his servant's amazement, Mr. Fogg gave some money to a beggar woman. At the station, Fogg met his five friends. "Well, gentlemen," said Fogg, "I'm off. If you examine my passport when I get back, you will be able to judge whether I have accomplished the journey agreed upon." "Oh, that would be quite unnecessary, Mr. Fogg," said Ralph politely. "We will trust your word, as you are a man of honour." Mr. Fogg bid them adieu as the train began whirling through Sydenham.

Soon enough every newspaper carried the news of Fogg's journey. *The Times, The Standard, Morning Post* and *Daily News* thought that Fogg's project was but a complete madness. *The Daily Telegraph* alone seemed to be supporting him with a certain hesitation.

As the news became the talk of the town, not just the members of the Reform Club, but even the general public began to make heavy wages for or against Phileas Fogg. "Phileas Fogg bonds" were offered at par or at premium on the Stock Exchange, and a great business was done in them. But when the Royal Geographical Society published an article in its bulletin expressing a lack of faith in the project, the demand began to subside.

Fix Gets Suspicious about Fogg

Amidst all the discussions about Mr. Fogg's adventure, a telegram reached the Commissioner of Police's office stating that Phileas Fogg was suspected of the recent bank robbery and an arrest warrant must be issued against him and dispatched to Bombay immediately. And this telegram was signed by Fix, a detective.

Thereby began a stir in the police department. A photograph of Mr. Fogg taken from the Reform Club was examined and a quite close match was found to the description of the gentleman who had robbed the bank.

On further investigation they found that Phileas Fogg's peculiar habits and his sudden departure simply helped to explain the robbery all the more. And they concluded that Fogg had made the wager with his friends at the Reform Club just to escape from England.

The circumstances under which the telegraphic dispatch was sent over were rather strange. The steamer

'Mongolia' was due at eleven o'clock in the morning on Wednesday, 9th of October at Suez. The British Consul and detective Fix were chatting on the wharves at Suez.

"The Mongolia, sir, has been in advance of the time required by the company's regulations, and gained the prize awarded for excess of speed," said the Consul at Fix's growing impatience.

"But really, I don't see how, from the description you have, you will be able to recognize your man, even if he is on board the Mongolia," he wondered.

"A man rather feels the presence of these fellows, Consul, than recognizes them. You must have a scent for them, like a sixth sense. I've arrested more than one of these gentlemen in my time, and, if my thief is on board, he'll not slip through my fingers," said Fix smugly.

Just then, amid sharp whistles, the 'Mongolia' entered the port and the Consul left for his office. Passengers began descending the 'Mongolia' and Fix as a habit began surveying them for the thief. One of them came up to him and asked the way to the British Consulate's office so that he could get his master's passport visaed. Fix examined the passport. It was alarming to see that the description matched the man he was looking for.

"Is your master on board?" Fix inquired. "Yes, he very much is," Passepartout replied.

"Then sir, I am afraid it is mandatory that he comes to the Consulate in person to get the visa." Passepartout left to inform his master while Fix himself went to the Consulate to notify the Consul of his concern with the passport he had just encountered.

"We must hold this man here until the arrest warrant arrives," said Fix. But the Consul's condition didn't seem to favour him. "I'd have to issue a visa, sir, if the passport is genuine. It is up to you how you wish to hold him here," said the Consul.

And at that instant both Mr. Fogg and Passepartout entered the office. Even though he could have entered Bombay without a visa as India continued to be under British rule, Mr. Fogg had to obtain it to prove that he came by Suez. The Consul proceeded to sign and date the passport, after which he added his official seal. Mr. Fogg paid the customary fee, coldly bowed, and went out, followed by his servant.

"Well, he looks like a perfectly honest man to me," said the Consul. "Somehow I doubt it," retorted Fix. "I will get the servant to talk. He is a Frenchman after all." And he went out in search of Passepartout.

Meanwhile, Phileas Fogg descended into his cabin aboard the 'Mongolia' and began studying his notebook. He came to the conclusion that from the day he left London he had in total, spent 158 1/2 hours; 6 days and a half at Suez. And thus he tabulated it:

"Left London, Wednesday,

October 2nd 8-45 p.m."

"Reached Paris, Thursday,

October 3rd 7-30 a.m."

"Left Paris, Thursday, 8.40 a.m."

"Reached Turin, Friday,

October 4th 6-35 a.m."

"Left Turin, Friday, 7.20 a.m."

"Arrived at Brindese, Saturday,

October 5th, 4 p.m."

"Sailed on the Mongolia, Saturday, 5 p.m."

"Reached Suez, Wednesday,

October 9th, 11 a.m."

"Total number of hours spent, 158 and a half or in days, six days and a half."

Then he wrote these dates down in a table properly divided into columns, indicating the month, the day of the month, and the day for the stipulated and actual arrivals at each principal point– Paris, Brindese, Suez, Bombay, Calcutta, Singapore, Hong Kong, Yokohama, San Francisco, New York and London from the 2nd of October to the 21st December and giving a space for setting down the gain made or the loss suffered on arrival at each of those places. He then sat down to breakfast without wishing once to inspect the town.

Fix caught up with Passepartout as he was lounging, looking out at the quay. "Well my friend, is your passport visaed?" he politely asked.

"It is. Thank you for asking," said Passepartout. Passepartout could not believe how fast they had been travelling. They had reached Africa already when he thought he'd not see beyond Paris.

"You are in great hurry then," said Fix. "I am not, but my Master is. Excuse me sir, I must go and buy some shoes and shirts. My master would be very cross if we missed the steamer," said Passepartout.

"You wouldn't miss it. It is just twelve o'clock. I know a place where you may buy good shoes and shirts. Let me show you," offered Fix. But Passepartout exclaimed at the time, "Twelve! why, it's only eight minutes before ten."

"You have kept London time," said Fix, "You ought to regulate your watch at noon in each country."

"I regulate my watch? Never!"

"Well then, it will not agree with the sun."

"So much the worse for the sun, monsieur!"

After a few moments of silence, Fix continued, "You left London in a hurry?"

"Quite. Last Friday at eight o'clock, Monsieur Fogg came home from his club, and forty-five minutes later we were off," Passepartout said.

"But where is your master going?"

"He is going around the world. Yes, and in eighty days! He says it is on a wager, but I don't believe it," Passepartout went on.

"Is he rich?" probed Fix.

"No doubt, for he is carrying an enormous sum of brand new bank notes with him." Passepartout had no idea what effects this innocent statement might have on him and his master's well being.

Fix was beginning to get what he wanted. "Have you known your master for long?" He went on relentlessly. "Why no; I entered his service the very day we left London." Passepartout and Fix had now reached the shop. Fix left him to make his purchases, and hurried back to the Consulate. He had come to a definite conclusion.

Fix Journeys by the Ship 'Mongolia'

They had left London in a hurry and were going around the world carrying with them an enormous amount of brand new bank notes. Fix found himself staring in disbelief.

He immediately went to the Consul and told him that Fogg was indeed the bank robber and wanted him to send a dispatch to London for a warrant of arrest to be sent instantly to Bombay. The warrant he expected would reach Bombay on the same day as Mongolia and since it was British soil he would be able to arrest Fogg.

Among the passengers on board the 'Mongolia', there were officials and military officers of various ranks. Fogg found partners in the Rev. Decimus Smith and a Brigadier General for a game of whist. Passepartout was pleased to find Fix on the deck and struck ready company. Fix misled Passepartout to believe that he was an agent of the Peninsular Company.

The 'Mongolia' moved on rapidly and passed Mocha on the 13th, strait of Babel, Mandel on the 14th and steamer point for coal on the 15th. On Sunday, the 20th of October the Indian Coast was sighted and at half-past four, the ship reached Bombay. It had reached on the 20th, two days early of the scheduled date. This was a gain to Phileas Fogg since his departure from London, and he calmly entered the fact in the itinerary, in the column of gains.

Passepartout was
Beaten inside the Pagoda

The great Indian Peninsular Railway from Bombay to Calcutta took three days and had more than 1,300 miles to traverse. Leaving Bombay it would go over the Western Ghats, to reach Burhampoor and then Allahabad before turning east, and passing through Benares and Burdwan, and finally Chandernagore to reach Calcutta.

The passengers of 'Mongolia' went ashore at half past four and exactly at eight, the train was to leave for Calcutta. After giving his servant some errands to do, Fogg walked through the city to the Passport Office, least interested in the wonders of Bombay—its famous city hall, its splendid library, its forts and docks, its bazaars, mosques, synagogues, Armenian churches and the noble pagoda on Malabar Hill, with its two polygonal towers. Settling his business at the Passport Office he went straight to the diner at the railway station and ordered dinner.

On the other hand, detective Fix after de-boarding went straight to the Bombay police and after producing

his proof of identity asked whether a warrant had arrived from London. Sorely disappointed to learn that it had not arrived, Fix attempted to get one from the Director of Bombay Police himself. But that was not to be. Therefore, he resolved to keep an eye on Phileas Fogg while he was in Bombay.

Meanwhile, Passepartout, after buying the shoes and shirts as he was told, was taking a stroll when he spotted the grand pagoda on the Malabar hill. Passepartout had a sudden desire to see its interior. He went inside but he did not know that Christians were forbidden to enter the premises. Standing in the middle of the Pagoda, Passepartout began admiring the ornamentation when suddenly three Brahmin priests pounced upon him, tore his shoes off and began to beat him while shouting at him angrily. But the agile Passepartout knocked down two of his adversaries and dodged the third one. The nimble Frenchman then rushed out of the Pagoda and escaped his pursuers by mingling with the crowd in the streets.

Passepartout, hatless, shoeless, and having in the squabble lost his package of shirts and shoes, rushed breathlessly to the station just five minutes before eight. Fix, who had followed Fogg to the station, noticed that Fogg was about to leave Bombay. He was watching Mr. Fogg closely, hidden in an obscure corner when Passepartout, without noticing him there, narrated his tale to his master between gasps for breath.

But Fix heard it all. He was glad that an offence had been committed on Indian soil and now he could arrest both of them on that pretext.

An Elephant as a Means of Conveyance

On train to Benares, Passepartout sat along with his master, and a third passenger, Sir Francis Comarty. Mr. Fogg had often played whist with Sir Francis on the Mongolia.

Sir Francis was now on his way to join his corps at Benares. He was a tall, fair man of fifty, who had distinguished himself in the Sepoy Revolt. The train soon passed Salsette, then Khandalah and entered Poona. Mountains and forests passed by and after Nasik, and then Khandesh, at half-past twelve it stopped at Burhampoor for a quick breakfast. It then resumed its course and crossed the Satpura range and suddenly halted.

It was eight o'clock and the train had stopped in the middle of a glade. The conductor announced loudly, "Passengers will get down here!" A surprised Mr. Fogg looked at Sir Francis for an explanation. The general stepped out to enquire.

"In the village of Kholby, sir," the conductor replied.

"Do we stop here?"

"Certainly. The railway isn't finished yet."

"But the papers announced the opening of the railway throughout."

"The papers were mistaken. There's still fifty miles of line to be laid from here to Allahabad."

"Yet you sell tickets to this train from Bombay to Calcutta," retorted Sir Francis, agitated.

"The passengers know they must provide means of transport for themselves from Kholby to Allahabad, sir," the conductor explained.

"Sir Francis," said Fogg, "we will look about for some means of conveyance." But after searching the village from end to end, they came back without finding anything. Passepartout suddenly joined his master, "Monsieur, I have found a means of conveyance." "What?" exclaimed Sir Francis, amazed.

"An elephant!" Passepartout said with a grimace.

"Let's go and see it," Mr. Fogg volunteered.

They soon reached a small hut near which, enclosed within a fence was the animal. An Indian came out of the hut, and upon their request guided them inside the enclosure. 'Kiouni', the elephant could travel rapidly for a long time, and because he had no other choice, Fogg resolved to hire him. But when he put forward his proposal of hiring the beast for ten pounds, the Indian flatly refused. Fogg then proposed to purchase the animal outright and after much bargaining over the price, the Indian sold it to him for 2,000 pounds.

As regarding a guide, a young Parsi fitted the bill over and he made the necessary modifications on the elephant's back for comfortable travel. Soon the elephant set forth with Fogg on one side and the General on the other with Passepartout in the middle. The Parsi was perched on the elephant's neck and the adventure started at 9 o'clock that evening.

Fogg Gets a Social Cause to Fight for

After a couple of hours the guide stopped to give the animal some rest. Kiouni was fed and watered and the journey resumed across dense forests, dry plains and much of Bundelkhand - notorious for its fanatical Hindu populace.

At eight in the evening they halted at a ruined bungalow and as it was cold, a fire was lit and dinner was served. The party rested for the night.

The journey resumed at six in the morning and when they had reached a dense forest, the elephant stopped suddenly confused with some concert of human noises accompanied by brass instruments. The Parsi guide jumped down, tied the elephant and urged the others to hide themselves to avoid being seen by the procession.

The procession soon came to sight, led by some Brahmin priests in long robes followed by folks singing a mournful psalm. Behind them a car followed carrying a statue which Sir Francis instantly identified as of Goddess Kali- the Hindu Goddess of love and death. Some old Fakirs who had cuts on their bodies followed her while blood oozed from their wounds. Some Brahmins led a woman. She was fair and young, grandly adorned with gold and jewels and seemed to be intoxicated. She was followed by some fierce looking guards. Sabers and pistols hung from their belts. They carried the corpse of an old rajah in a palanquin heavily decorated with jewels.

"A Suttee," Sir Francis whispered. The Parsi nodded and pressed a finger to his lips.

The procession was soon lost from view and the music faded. Phileas Fogg was curious. "What is a Suttee?" He asked.

"A Suttee," replied the general, "is a human sacrifice. The woman you have just seen will be burned alive."

"And the corpse?" asked Mr. Fogg scandalized. "That is of the Prince, her husband," replied the guide, "an independent rajah of Bundelkhand."

"If she were not burned alive," said Francis, "you cannot conceive what treatment she would get from her relatives. They would shave off her hair, feed her on a scanty allowance of rice, and treat her with utter contempt."

"Is it possible," resumed Phileas Fogg, "that these barbarous customs still exist in India, and that the English have been unable to put a stop to them?"

"The government has declared it as illegal. Sometimes, when the sacrifice is voluntary, it requires

the active interference of the government to prevent it."

The guide shook his head, and said, "This sacrifice is not a voluntary one. Everyone knows about this affair in Bundelkhand."

"But she did not offer any resistance," observed Fogg.

"That is because they have drugged her," said the guide.

"But where are they taking her?"

"Two miles from here, to the pagoda of Pillaji. She will pass the night there. The sacrifice will take place at the first light of dawn."

Fogg said turning to Sir Francis, "Suppose we save this woman?"

"Save the woman, Mr. Fogg!"

"I have twelve hours to spare."

"Why, you are a man of heart!" exclaimed Sir Francis. "Sometimes," replied Phileas Fogg quietly, "when I have the time."

Mr. Fogg was going to risk his life, or at least his liberty, and therefore the success of his tour. He found that Sir Francis too was enthusiastic about it. As for Passepartout, he was ready for anything that his master suggested. There remained the guide. Sir Francis put the question to him. He said, "Sir, I am a Parsi, and this woman is also a Parsi. I will follow as you command." And they decided to wait until the nightfall.

Saving the Lady from Being a Suttee

The guide told them more about the lady who was being led to commit 'Suttee'. Her name was Aouda. She was a much celebrated beauty of the Parsi community and the daughter of a wealthy Bombay merchant. She had received an English education in that city, and from her manners and intelligence, she seemed like a European.

But when fate took away her parents, she was forcibly married to the old rajah of Bundelkhand, and when the rajah died, she escaped, knowing what was waiting for her. But the rajah's relatives, who would benefit from her death had somehow retraced her and were now forcing her to commit 'Suttee'.

The elephant was directed to the pagoda from where the cries of the Fakirs could be heard. The abduction was to be made at night. At nightfall, the guide led the others towards the pagoda but they were disappointed as the rajah's guards guarded the tents with sabers in their hands. The group drew back and decided to wait.

After what seemed like several hours, and the guards remained awake, another plan to make an opening in one of the walls of the pagoda was thought of. It was easy work to make a hole when suddenly cries were heard from the inside of the pagoda. Fearing an alarm, the group quickly ran back into the woods. As the hours continued to pass, the horizon lit with dawn. Suddenly Passepartout had an idea!

The tambourines sounded and songs and cries rose. The hour of sacrifice had come. The doors of the Pagoda opened and the woman was seen in the middle. As the procession began to move, Fogg and his group followed. They reached the river bank where a pyre was made. The woman, very intoxicated was stretched along with her husband's corpse and a torch was lit.

Suddenly, to everyone's horror, the old rajah sprang alive. He carried his wife in his arms and fled the spot.

It was Passepartout who had disguised himself as the rajah and lay on the pyre. The procession was stunned and confused and they bowed with their face down on the ground believing that it was some divine activity. Mr. Fogg and his rescue team on the elephant, took this opportunity and quickly disappeared into the forest with the woman.

The elephant in the guidance of the Parsi was advancing rapidly through the forest. Aouda, now wrapped in a blanket, was still unconscious. Sir Francis pressed Passepartout's hand and congratulated him.

"Well done!" Mr. Fogg said. Passepartout, humbled by the appreciation, knew that the credit of the affair belonged to Mr. Fogg. He had realized that fortune indeed favoured the brave.

Reaching Calcutta with Aouda

They reached Allahabad station at ten o'clock. If they could reach Calcutta within a day, then Fogg would be able to take the steamer for Hong Kong that left on October 25 at noon. While Aouda stayed at the waiting room of the station, Passepartout was sent to purchase clothing and toiletries for her.

Aouda was a charming woman. She spoke English with great ease and was very beautiful. The guide had not exaggerated when he said that the young Parsi woman was brought up in accordance with European ways.

Just as the train was about to leave Allahabad station, Fogg offered the elephant to the guide as a token of appreciation for his service and devotion. The guide accepted it and was very happy. The train moved swiftly and covering a distance of eighty miles in two hours, reached Benares. During the journey, Aouda had recovered from her intoxication. She was amazed to find herself alive and in a train carriage with strangers. Sir Francis told her what had happened the night before. Aouda was overwhelmed with gratitude.

Fogg assured Aouda that he would escort her to Hong Kong, where Aouda's relative - a wealthy Parsi merchant lived. At half past twelve, the train stopped at Benares and Sir Francis got down wishing Mr. Fogg all the success in the world. The train moved on and soon passed the Gangetic valley of Bihar which was spread with neat villages, fields of wheat and corn and thick forests. Elephants and men bathed in the rivers. Soon Ghazipur, and the fort town of Buxar and Patna were sighted. They reached Calcutta via Cornwallis' tomb, at seven in the morning.

Fogg and Passepartout, Both Sentenced

When they were about to leave the station, a policeman came up to Mr. Fogg and asked whether he was Phileas Fogg and pointing to Passepartout asked whether he was his servant. The policeman then asked them to follow him and soon they reached a court. Mr. Fogg and Passepartout were shocked to find out that they had been taken as prisoners. Aouda blamed herself, "You must have left me to my fate sir. It is because of me that they have arrested you." But Mr. Fogg felt otherwise. It was unlikely that they would be arrested for preventing a Suttee.

At 8.30, they were produced before the court of judge Obadiah. After the preliminaries were over, Passepartout demanded to know their crime. At this moment the door opened and three Indian priests entered.

The clerk read out a complaint of sacrilege against Mr. Fogg and his butler. They were accused of having violated a sacred place of the Hindus.

"You admit it?" asked the judge.

"Yes, I admit it if they admit theirs in turn," Mr. Fogg said.

Puzzled the priests looked at each other. "Yes," Passepartout cried out.

Passepartout told the court that these priests were forcing a woman to become a 'suttee'. "Did this happen in Bombay itself?" the judge was confused. Passepartout was surprised at the mention of Bombay. The clerk clarified that the case concerned the Pagoda at Malabar Hill in Bombay. As evidence he brought out the culprit's shoes, the ones Passepartout had left behind in a hurry to get away.

Both Mr. Fogg and Passepartout had forgotten their adventure at Bombay, when Passepartout had mistakenly entered the Pagoda at Malabar Hill and got involved in a fight with the priests. Detective Fix was sure that the English authorities dealt severely with this kind of misdemeanor. He had sent the priests to Calcutta in the next train, promising them a good reward. Had Passepartout looked around he would have noticed the detective watching the proceedings from a corner of the court-room.

The judge asked if the facts were true and Fogg pleaded guilty. Passepartout was sentenced to a fifteen-day imprisonment and a fine of three hundred pounds whereas as his master, Mr. Fogg was sentenced to a week's imprisonment and a fine of one hundred

and fifty pounds. Fix rubbed his hands softly with satisfaction. It was enough time to hold Fogg in Calcutta before the warrant arrived.

But just as the clerk was about to call the next case, Mr. Fogg rose, and said, "I offer bail." The judge agreed. "You have the right," he said.

Fix's blood ran cold. But when the judge announced that each prisoner would have to pay one thousand pounds as bail, he resumed his composure.

Fix hoped that the robber would not leave the 2,000 pounds behind him, but would decide to serve out his week in jail.

"I will pay it at once" said Fogg, taking a roll of notes from the carpet bag, and placing them on the clerk's desk.

"This sum will be restored to you upon your release from prison," said the judge. "Meanwhile you are liberated on bail."

"Come, let us go" Mr. Fogg said to Passepartout. And the determined gentleman took a carriage, and the party soon landed on one of the quays. Fix saw them leaving the carriage and pushing off in a boat for the steamer called 'Rangoon'.

Fogg's Party Reaches Hong Kong

Aouda began to get acquainted with Mr. Fogg and Passepartout. She indeed belonged to the family of Sir Jametsee Jeejeebhoy who had made great fortunes in India by dealing in cotton and was made a baronet by the English government. It was his cousin, Jeejeeh, whom she hoped to join in Hong Kong. Mr. Fogg promised her that he would make sure she reached her relatives safely.

The trip from Calcutta to Hong Kong took some ten to twelve days and covered a distance of three thousand five hundred miles. The weather was good as they passed the Andaman Islands. Fix, after leaving orders that if the warrant arrived, it should be sent to him in Hong Kong, had got on to the 'Rangoon' at Calcutta without being seen by Passepartout.

He began wondering what must have happened that now a young beautiful woman accompanied Mr. Fogg and Passepartout on their journey around the world. Fix could no longer control his curiosity.

On October 30, he came out of his cabin and went on to the deck where Passepartout was enjoying the air.

Passepartout was surprised to see Fix on board. "Are you going around the world too?" he asked. However, Fix replied that he was going to Hong Kong where he wished to stay for a few days.

Passepartout grew suspicious. He began to wonder why Fix was following the same route that his master was taking. And he soon found an explanation for it. He decided that Fix was an agent of Mr. Fogg's friends at the Reform Club, sent to make sure that Mr. Fogg really went around the world. However, he chose not to say anything to his master.

On 31st of October, at four in the morning, the ship reached Singapore gaining half a day; and at eleven o'clock, she was out of the harbour.

Fogg hoped to reach Hong Kong in six days so that he would be in time for the steamer which was to leave on the 6th of November for Yokohama.

But as they continued their journey from Singapore, he was disappointed to find that the weather had changed. The waves became monstrous, the ship rolled heavily and a storm arose. The steamer was forced to proceed slowly.

It was estimated that 'Rangoon' would reach Hong Kong a day late. But on 4th of November the sea calmed. But land remained out of sight until five o'clock on the morning of 6 November. Mr. Fogg was a day behind and he calculated that he would surely miss the steamer for Yokohama.

He approached the pilot of the ship and calmly asked him if the steamer for Yokohama had left already. "At high tide to-morrow morning," answered the pilot. "They had to repair one of her boilers, and so her departure was postponed till tomorrow," he added. Mr. Fogg thanked the pilot and retired to his cabin.

Mr. Fogg was in luck. Had the steamer to Yokohama – the 'Carnatic' left on its scheduled time, they would have had to wait a week before leaving for Japan.

At one o'clock the 'Rangoon' was docked. The 'Carnatic' was to leave Hong Kong at five, the next morning. On landing, Fogg and his party drove to the club hotel and rooms were engaged for Aouda. Fogg went in search of her relative but was told that Jeejeeh had left China two years ago and had settled in Holland. Fogg returned to the hotel and told Aouda about the situation. She was confused. "What do you suggest I do Mr. Fogg?" she asked. "You will come with us to Europe," Mr. Fogg said and he told Passepartout to buy three tickets on the 'Carnatic'.

Fix Discloses his Identity to Passepartout

At the quay, Passepartout was not astonished to find Fix pacing. He jokingly asked the detective, "Do you plan to come with us to America?" "Yes," Fix replied through gritted teeth.

They entered the steamer office and secured cabins for four persons. The clerk, as he gave them the tickets, informed them that, the repairs on the 'Carnatic' having been completed, the steamer would leave that very evening, and not next morning, as had been announced.

Fix had decided to tell Passepartout everything and so he invited him to a tavern on the quay. He decided that it was the only way he could hold Fogg in Hong Kong until the arrest warrant arrived.

On entering the tavern, they found themselves in a room at the end of which was a bed with cushions. Some people lay on the bed in a deep sleep. At the small tables arranged about the room, some thirsty customers were drinking beer, gin and brandy; smoking long red clay pipes stuffed with balls of opium. From time to time one of the smokers, overcome with the narcotic, would slip under the table. The waiters would then take him by the head and feet, carry and lay him upon the bed.

Fix ordered two bottles of port. When the bottles were empty, Passepartout rose to go and tell his master about the change in the Carnatic's schedule. Fix caught him by the arm, and said, "Wait a minute".

"What for, Mr. Fix?"

"What I have to say concerns your master. Have you guessed who I am?"

"I know everything!" replied Passepartout.

"You don't know how large the sum is."

"Of course I do, 20,000 pounds."

"A sum of 55,000 pounds".

"What! Monsieur Fogg has dared 55,000 pounds!" cried Passepartout, getting up hastily. Fix pushed Passepartout back in his chair and resumed, "A sum of 55,000. If I succeed, I get 2,000. If you help me keep Mr. Fogg here for three days, I'll let you have 500 of them."

"Members of the Reform Club!" cried Passepartout. "You know that my master is an honest man!"

"But who do you think I am?"

"Why, an agent of the members of the Reform Club, sent out here to interrupt my master's journey."

"Listen," said Fix quietly. "I am a police detective sent out from London. Here is my commission."

Fix displayed a document to prove it. Passepartout was speechless.

"Mr. Fogg's wager," continued Fix, "is only an excuse. He is only using his friends at the Reform Club and you as his alibi."

"But why?"

"On the 28th of September, a robbery of 55,000 pounds was committed at the Bank of England by a person whose description was fortunately found by the police. It matches exactly with that of Mr. Fogg."

"What nonsense!" cried Passepartout. "My master is the most honorable of men!"

"How can you tell? You hardly know anything about him. You went into his service the day he left London, carrying a large amount of bank notes."

Passepartout, overcome by what he had heard, held his head between his hands. Phileas Fogg, that brave and generous man, the saviour of Aouda, a thief?

"I have tracked Mr. Fogg to this place, but I have failed to receive the warrant of arrest from London. You must help me detain him here in Hong Kong, until it arrives," Fix said.

"Never!" replied Passepartout.

"You refuse? Alright. Consider that I've said nothing", said Fix; "let us drink!"

Passepartout felt himself yielding to the effects of the liquor. Some pipes of opium lay on the table. Fix slipped one into Passepartout's hands. He put it between his lips, lit it, drew several puffs, and, unconscious he fell upon the floor.

Had Mr. Fogg been capable of being astonished at anything, he would have been astonished to not see his servant return at bedtime. But, knowing that the steamer was not to leave for Yokohama until the next morning, he did not worry about the matter. When Passepartout did not appear the next morning, Mr. Fogg took his carpetbag, called Aouda, and sent for a rickshaw. It was eight o'clock. Half an hour later, they stepped upon the quay. Mr. Fogg learned that 'Carnatic' had sailed the evening before.

Gracefully Built Little Craft – The Tankadere

Fix who had been watching Fogg took the opportunity and approached him. "Were you not on board the 'Rangoon' like me, sir?" he asked Fogg trying to find a reason to talk to him. "Yes sir," Fogg replied, "But I do not have the honour of..."

"Pardon me sir, I was hoping to find your servant here," said Fix. "Do you know where he is?"

"I do not believe he has sailed away in the 'Carnatic' without us!" Aouda exclaimed, worried about Passepartout's absence.

"Yes, the 'Carnatic' did sail twelve hours before its time as its repairs were completed. We must now wait for a week for the next steamer to Yokohama," Fix's heart was leaping with joy as he said this to Fogg.

"There must be a boat we can hire," Fogg said calmly. Colour drained from Fix's face. There went his plan to detain Fogg.

Fogg went in search of other ships in the harbour along with Aouda with Fix behind them. After a few hours of search a sailor offered a fast pilot boat to

Mr. Fogg. When Fogg told the sailor about the proposed voyage to Yokohama, he was amazed and even though Fogg offered a good sum of money the sailor seemed unwilling at the proposal of such a long trip. But he agreed to take them to Shanghai - a distance of 800 miles from where the 'San Francisco' steamer started. They were told that the steamer left on the 11th at seven in the evening. Mr. Fogg decided to take the chance.

The sailor, John Bunsby, was the master of the Tankadere. The Tankadere was a little craft, as gracefully built as a racing yacht. It seemed capable of brisk speed. Her crew consisted of Bunsby and four mariners, who were familiar with the Chinese seas. Bunsby, a man of forty with an energetic and self-reliant countenance, would have inspired confidence in the most timid mind.

Fix, at Mr. Fogg's offer, joined them on the voyage. As Fogg, Aouda and Fix sat on Tankadere's deck, they wondered whether they would have to leave without the poor Passepartout. He was nowhere to be seen. As Bunsby the master, at length gave the orders, the Tankadere set off bounding on the waves.

A Journey of only a Hundred Miles

The 800 miles voyage was very adventurous. Bunsby told Fogg about an upcoming storm. At 8 o'clock, the storm came upon them accompanied by wind and rain. At night the tempest increased its violence. But the very next day, the storm had subsided and they had miraculously survived. That night it was comparatively calm and the boat kept up the good speed.

The next morning at dawn, they could see the coast, and Bunsby said that they were only hundred miles away from Shanghai. That very evening Fogg was due at Shanghai. Had there been no storm, they would have been within thirty miles from their destination. The wind grew calmer. All sails were now hoisted, and at noon the Tankadere was within forty-five miles of Shanghai. Thus remained six hours in which they were to cover that distance. But the wind was becoming calmer. Bunsby warned them of a typhoon that was approaching.

At seven they were still three miles from Shanghai. The breeze that was blowing from the coast began to

disrupt their speed. Bunsby was beginning to believe that the reward of two hundred pounds was going to be lost.

At this moment, a long black funnel, crowned with wreaths of smoke, appeared on the edge of the waters. It was the American steamer leaving for Yokohama. "Signal her!" cried Fogg desperately.

A small brass cannon stood on the forward deck of the Tankadere. It was loaded to the muzzle; but just as the master was about to apply a red hot coal to the touch-hole, Fogg cried, "Hoist your flag!" The flag was run at half mast, this being the signal of distress.

"Fire!" cried Fogg, and the booming of the little cannon resounded in the air.

Passepartout in a Circus Company

The signal made by the Tankadere was spotted by the captain of the Yokohama steamer who ordered his ship towards the little boat. Fogg rewarded Bunsby handsomely and ascended the steamer with Aouda and Fix. They reached Yokohama on the morning of the 14th of November. Fogg went aboard the 'Carnatic' where he was told that Passepartout had arrived on it the day before.

At dawn on the 13th, the 'Carnatic' had entered the port of Yokohama. Passepartout had gone ashore penniless and hungry inquiring about his master. The next morning he spotted a placard carried by a clown from a circus company and Passepartout immediately followed him in search of a job. Batulear, the proprietor told him that he had enough men already. But the determined Passepartout said he was strong, could sing and act like a clown. "But can you sing standing on your head, with a top spinning on your left foot, and a sabre balanced on your right?" the proprietor

asked. "I think so," Passepartout replied. So he was hired that very minute.

The show began and the large shed was invaded by spectators. Equilibrists and musicians; acrobats and jugglers showed their mastery. But the main attraction was the exhibition of long noses! These noses which were made of bamboo were five or six and even ten feet long! In the last scene a 'human' pyramid had been announced, in which fifty Long noses were to form a pyramid by grouping themselves on the top of the noses. It so happened that the performer who had hitherto formed the base of the pyramid had quitted the troupe.

Passepartout went upon the stage, and took his place beside the rest who were to compose the base of the pyramid. They all stretched themselves on the floor, their noses pointing to the ceiling. A second group perched themselves on these long appendages, then a third above these, then a fourth, until a human monument reaching to the very cornices of the theater soon arose.

This encouraged a loud applause, in the midst of which the orchestra began to play, when the pyramid tottered. The balance was lost as one of the lower noses had vanished. The human monument shattered. It was Passepartout's fault. Abandoning his position and, running up to the gallery, he fell at the feet of one of the spectators, crying, "Ah! My master! My master!"

"You here?" Fogg exclaimed. "Very well, let us hurry to the steamer, young man!"

Mr. Fogg had been wandering in the streets searching for his lost butler, and chance had led him into the Honorable Batulear's establishment. He certainly would not have recognised Passepartout in his costume; but the servant, lying on his back, had spotted his master in the gallery.

At half-past six, Fogg and Aouda, followed by Passepartout, who in his hurry had retained his wings and the six feet long nose, stepped upon the steamer. Passepartout apologized for having been overtaken by drunkenness at a tavern in Hong Kong as his master heard his narrative coldly, without a word.

Fix Apologizes

The steamer named 'General Grant' was well-equipped and swift. At a speed of twelve miles per hour she could cross the Pacific Ocean in twenty-one days. On the 9th day after leaving Yokohama, Fogg had covered half of the globe. 'General Grant' passed the 180th meridian and was at the very antipodes of London. Fogg had spent 52 of the 80 days but though he was half way by the difference of meridians, he had really gone over two-thirds of the whole journey; for he had been obliged to make long circuits from London to Aden, Aden to Bombay, Calcutta to Singapore and from Singapore to Yokohama.

If Fogg could have followed without deviation the 50th parallel which is that of London, the whole distance would have been 12000 miles. But because of various methods of transport he had to traverse 26000 miles of which he had on the 23rd of November accomplished 17,500.

On 23 November, Passepartout noticed Fix on the deck and he grabbed the detective by the collar and thrashed him. Fix apologized and told him that he

would support Fogg's adventure and remove all the obstacles out of his way until they reached England when it would be known whether Mr. Fogg was a criminal or an honest man. Finally, on 3 December, the General Grant entered the bay of the Golden Gate, and reached San Francisco.

Mr. Fogg had neither gained nor lost a single day.

Back to America

At seven in the morning, Fogg and his party landed in America. Fogg immediately went to the Railway station and learnt that the first train to New York would leave at six in the evening. They took a horse-carriage and went to the International Hotel.

After breakfast, Fogg left for the Consulate to have his passport visaed. On the way, he met Passepartout who suggested that they should buy some rifles as protection against the Sioux and Pawnees. Though Mr. Fogg thought it was useless, he agreed and left for the Consulate.

A little later Fogg met Fix who requested him to accompany in his walk around San Francisco. Mr. Fogg accepted and they walked. At Montgomery Street, they saw a huge crowd carrying large posters. Suspecting it to be a political meeting the two sensed danger and they decided to return to the hotel.

At the station in the evening, before boarding the train, Fogg asked a porter about the disturbance on the streets that day.

"It was a political meeting, sir," replied the porter.

"A meeting assembled for an election."

"The election of a general-in-chief, no doubt?" asked Mr. Fogg.

"No, sir; of a Justice of the peace."

Mr. Fogg got into the train and they set off towards their destination.

Beginning of Pacific Railroad Journey

The Pacific Railroad was divided into two lines: the Central Pacific, between San Francisco and Ogden and the Union Pacific, between Ogden and Omaha. Five mainlines connect Omaha with New York. New York and San Francisco were thus united by an uninterrupted metal ribbon of no less than 3,786 miles. The car, which Fogg and his party occupied, was an omnibus on eight wheels, with no compartments in the interior. It had two rows of seats on either side of an aisle which led to the front and rear platforms. These platforms were joined throughout, and the passengers were able to pass from one end of the train to the other.

The train left Oakland station at six o'clock. Soon it began to snow. From San Francisco to Sacramento - a distance of 120 miles - it took six hours. They reached Cisco at seven in the morning and at nine o'clock, the train entered the state of Nevada through the Carson valley. At mid-day, they stopped at Reno for breakfast. From this point the road ran along the banks of the Humboldt River for several miles. Fogg and his partners observed the varied landscape, which unfolded itself as they passed along the vast prairies, the mountains lining the horizon, and the creeks in their frothy, foaming streams.

At 12 noon some 12,000 buffaloes encumbered the track. It took nearly three hours to get the track cleared.

At half past nine, the train reached Utah and then Ogden at two o'clock on 6 December, where it halted for six hours. Later, the train headed for the Wasatch Mountains. This was the most difficult part of the track. From this point railway described a long curve descending towards bitter creek valley. There were many creeks in this mountainous region and it was necessary to cross them upon culverts.

Crossing the Shaky Bridge at Full Speed

At 11 in the morning, on the 7th of December, the train had reached Bridger Pass about 7,000 feet above sea-level. At half past twelve, they could see Fort Hallock and in a few hours, the rocky mountains were crossed.

Mr. Fogg and his partners were playing whist, when suddenly, the train stopped before a red signal. The signal-man was heard saying that the bridge at Medicine Bow was shaky and would not bear the weight of the train. "We have telegraphed to Omaha for a train, but it is not likely that it will reach Medicine Bow in less than six hours," said the conductor. "Six hours?" cried Passepartout. The other passengers seemed agitated. They could not cross the river on a boat because the creek had swollen by the rains.

An engineer named Forster said, "Gentlemen, we have a chance of crossing the bridge. I think that by putting on the very highest speed we might have a chance of getting over." The conductor was astonished.

However, despite his warning the eager passengers boarded the train attracted by this proposal.

After reversing nearly for a mile, the train began to pick-up speed and went forward at a great pace of hundred miles per hour, they crossed the bridge. No sooner had they passed, when the bridge crashed onto the rapids of Medicine Bow.

A Duel between Proctor and Fogg

The train soon passed Fort Sanders, crossed Cheyenne Pass and reached Evans Pass. This was about 8,000 feet above sea-level. They entered Nebraska at eleven, Fort McPherson was crossed at eight in the morning; and another 357 miles separated them from Omaha.

Fogg and his partners had resumed their game of whist when they heard a voice from behind, which turned out to be Colonel Stamp Proctor's. Proctor began provoking Fogg but Fix got up saying it was he who had a score to settle with Proctor. Fogg restrained him saying that as it was a matter between him and Proctor, he would deal with it. A duel was proposed and Proctor suggested an exchange of revolver fire. Fogg agreed. He then returned to the car to reassure Aouda, and asked Fix to be his second at the duel.

At eleven they were at Plum Creek. But just as the combatants were about to step down from the train, the conductor shouted, "You can't get off here. We are twenty minutes behind, and we shall not stop."

The train had already started. "Why not fight along as we go?" he asked.

The two combatants, their seconds and the conductor passed through the cars to the rear of the train. The last car had a dozen passengers, whom the conductor politely asked to vacate, as the two gentlemen had an affair to settle. The passengers granted the request.

Fogg and Colonel Proctor, each provided with two six-barreled revolvers, entered the car. They were to begin firing at the first whistle of the locomotive. They were listening for the whistle, when suddenly savage cries resounded in the air, accompanied by the reports which did not issue from the car where they were.

The train was being attacked by a band of Sioux, some of whom had already invaded the cars. A Sioux chief, wishing to stop the train, but not knowing how to work the regulator, had opened wide instead of closing the steam valve, and the locomotive was plunging forward with terrific velocity.

The travellers defended themselves bravely; some of the cars were barricaded, and sustained a siege, like moving forts carried along at a speed of 100 miles an hour. The conductor cried out: "Unless the train is stopped in five minutes, we are lost!"

"I will go," said Passepartout. Opening a door, unperceived by the Indians, he slipped under the car. Holding on to the chains, creeping from one car to another, he gained the forward end of the train. There, suspended by one hand between the baggage car and the tender, with the other he loosened the safety chains; but, owing to the traction, he would never have succeeded in unscrewing the yoking bar, had not a violent concussion jolted this bar out.

The train, now detached from the engine, remained a little behind, whilst the locomotive rushed forward. They stopped less than hundred feet from Fort Kearney station. The soldiers of the fort, attracted by the shots, hurried up; the Sioux had not expected them, and decamped in a body before the train stopped entirely.

When the passengers counted each other on the platform, several were found missing; among others the courageous Frenchman, whose devotion had just saved them.

Fogg Shows his Courage

Fogg had to rescue Passepartout. But this meant that he would have to miss the steamer at New York. He did not mind. His duty was to save the brave Passepartout. When he suggested this to the Fort's officer, he was reluctant to send 50 men to rescue the lives of three. But when Fogg decided to go alone, the officer was moved and soon the whole company was eager to join.

Fogg pressed Aouda's hand, and having confided to her, his precious carpetbag, went off with the little squad. At a little past noon, she retired to the waiting room, thinking of Mr. Fogg's courage. Around two o'clock whistles were heard from the east. The locomotive which had been detached from the train entered the station. It had continued its route with terrific speed, carrying off the unconscious engineer and stoker. It had finally stopped an hour after twenty miles beyond Fort Kearney.

The engineer when he found himself in the desert, and the locomotive without cars, understood what had happened. He began to rebuild the fire in the furnace;

the pressure mounted again, and it returned, running backwards to Fort Kearney. The travelers were glad to see the locomotive resume its place at the head of the train. Soon they boarded the train and it left the station.

It was evening, and yet there was no news of Fogg and his men. Everyone was tense with anxiety. At dawn, they suddenly saw Fogg leading his men along with Passepartout and the other two passengers. Fogg was twenty hours behind schedule. At this, Fix suggested traversing on a sledge! Only then could they make any advance.

Moving on in a Sledge

The sledge could carry atleast 6 people. A high mast was fixed and a large sail was attached to it. A kind of ruddier served to guide the vehicle. During winters, when the railroad was blocked up by snow, these sledges were used to make rapid journeys across frozen plains.

Fogg made a deal with Mudge, owner of the sledge. At eight they started, cloaked in thick coats. At a speed of 40 miles an hour with Omaha 200 miles away, it was an exciting but dangerous journey. But Mudge was careful and they managed to reach Omaha.

Fogg and his group reached the station and were just in time to board the train to Chicago. The train passed Sowa, and on December 10th reached Chicago, at 4 in the evening. New York was 900 miles away but as trains were plentiful, they got onto one and it went on full speed. It soon passed Indiana, Ohio and later Pennsylvania. Soon enough New Jersey was crossed and at eleven in the night on the 11th of December, they reached New York. But unfortunately the steamer

'China' that went to Liverpool had left 45 minutes earlier.

Fix Arrests Fogg

It seemed that Fogg's hopes were smashed. As no other steamer was in sight, they crossed the Hudson river and took a room for the night. The next morning on 12th of December, Fogg reached the Port and upon searching the boats, he chanced upon a trading vessel called 'Henrietta', captained by Andrew Speedy of Cardiff.

Fogg spoke to Speedy about the viability of going to Boardeaux and after some discussion, Speedy agreed to take them at 2000 dollars per person. Fogg agreed. The captain thought it was a good deal. The next day Fogg boarded the 'Henrietta' and after bribing Speedy's milling sailors, they managed to lock the captain in his room and directed the boat towards Liverpool!

Initially, it was smooth sailing but on the 16th, the Engineer became worried that the coal supply would not last till Liverpool. But Fogg was calm. Then on the 18th the Engineer said that the coal would get over that day itself! Captain Speedy was released by Fogg and was placated when Fogg told him that he wanted to buy the ship. This was so because it was necessary

to burn the upper parts to feed the fire. The angry captain was confused but gladly agreed for a sum of 60,000 dollars. It was a great bargain. But both Fix and Passepartout were highly surprised.

Soon the seats, bunks and frames were pulled down and burnt. The next day, the poop, cabins and the spare deck were sacrificed. On the 19th, the masts were burnt and by 20 December, the 'Henrietta' was on coast.

Only a flat hulk. That day, they sighted the Irish. Finally the 'Henrietta' entered Queenstown Harbour at one in the morning.

They all got upon the train at half-past one and at dawn were in Dublin. Fogg and his company got down at Liverpool at twenty minutes before 12, the 21st of December. He still had six hours to reach London.

Everything was well, when suddenly Fix announced that he was arresting Fogg! It was as if they were struck by thunder.

Fogg Makes it Home

Fogg was in prison. Aouda and Passepartout were shocked and dismayed. It was impossible that Fogg could be the bank robber. Fogg was impassive in his cell. At thirty-three minutes past two, the door flung open and Mr. Fogg saw Passepartout, Aouda, and Fix, who hurried towards him. Fix was out of breath. "Sir," he stammered, "sir, forgive me—most—unfortunate resemblance—robber arrested three days ago—you are free!"

Phileas Fogg was free! He walked to the detective, looked him steadily in the face, and with the only rapid motion knocked him down. "Well hit!" cried Passepartout, "Parbleu! that's what you might call a good application of English fists!"

Fix, who found himself on the floor, did not utter a word.

Soon, Fogg, Aouda and Passepartout got onto a cab and arrived at the station at 45 minutes past two. But only at three, they could start for London. On the way, there were some forced delays and so they could reach London at only ten minutes before nine. Having

completed the tour of the World, Fogg was late by 5 minutes! He had lost the wager.

Fogg was calm in his loss. After undertaking a long journey, overcoming a hundred obstacles, braving many dangers, he had failed the goal by a sudden event because he could not foresee his arrest.

A room at Fogg's house was set apart for Aouda, who was overwhelmed with grief at her protector's misfortune. The night passed. Aouda did not once close her eyes. Passepartout watched all night at his master's door.

The next day (Sunday) Fogg, for the first time since he had lived in the house, did not set out for the club when the Westminster clock struck half-past eleven. About half-past seven in the evening, Fogg sat down at the fireplace opposite Aouda, for several minutes, without speaking. Finally, he said, "When I decided to bring you here, I was rich, and counted on putting a portion of my fortune at your disposal; then you would have been happy and free. But now I am ruined."

"Will you forgive me for having followed you, and for having delayed you, and thus contributing to your ruin?"

"Madam, your safety could only be assured by bringing you to such a distance."

"They say that misery shared by two sympathetic souls, may be borne with patience Mr. Fogg" said Aouda, rising and seizing his hand; "Do you wish a

kinswoman and friend? Will you have me for your wife?" At this, Fogg rose in his turn. There was a slight trembling on his lips. The sincerity, firmness and sweetness of this noble woman, who could dare all to save him left him astonished.

"Yes," he said. "By all that is holiest, I love you, and I am yours."

Passepartout was summoned and told to notify the parish as the wedding was slated for the next day, Monday.

The Miscalculated Blessing

On the evening of 21 December, a great crowd had gathered at Pall Mall on anticipation of Fogg's arrival. The five gentlemen from the Reform Club were waiting for Mr. Fogg. When the clock struck 20 minutes past 8 pm, Stuart said that if Fogg's name was not on the list of the 'China', he must have failed to make it. They were waiting for the time to pass and win their bet. Slowly, the minutes began ticking away.

At 8:45 pm, a loud cry could be suddenly heard from the streets. Mr. Fogg had arrived!

Yes, the reader needs to recall that at half past eight in the evening, Passepartout had been sent by Fogg to engage the services of the Rev. Samuel Wilson to conduct a marriage ceremony; it was to take place the next day. When Passepartout finally managed to meet the Reverend, it was thirty-five minutes past eight.

Suddenly, he took leave from the Reverend, ran back to his master and began blabbering. It seemed that the next day was a Sunday and not Monday as Mr. Fogg had assumed. The Reverend, much to Passepartout's amazement had said that the marriage could not take

place on a Sunday. Passepartout realized that they had arrived on Saturday that is, twenty-four hours before they were scheduled to arrive! However, now only ten minutes were left before Mr. Fogg could claim his winnings.

Passepartout and Fogg dashed to the Reform Club in a cab and managed somehow to reach at 8:45 that evening. It was strange that Fogg, who was known for his exactness and fastidiousness, had miscalculated!

He had all along gathered one day on his journey and this was because he had constantly travelled Eastward. There were 360 degrees on the circumference of the earth; there are 360 degrees multiplied by 4 minutes, that gives precisely 24 hours - the day unconsciously gained. Fogg had won 20,000 pounds but as he had spent nearly 19,000 on the way, the monetary gain was small. He divided this between Passepartout and Fix.

The marriage took place two days later. Passepartout was given the honour of giving the bride away. Phileas Fogg had made his journey around the world in 80 days. He had employed every means of conveyance - steamers, railways, carriages, yachts, trading vessels, sledges, elephants. And he had gained a charming woman who made him the happiest of men.